# What Happens Under the Hood?

by Barbara Lieff Fierman

## HOUGHTON MIFFLIN HARCOURT

**PHOTOGRAPHY CREDITS:** COVER ©Nancy Honey/Getty Images; 3 (b) ©Car Culture/Getty Images; 8 (b) ©Nancy Honey/Getty Images; 10 (b) ©Car Culture/Getty Images; 13 (b) ©Simon Clay/Alamy Images

Copyright © by Houghton Mifflin Harcourt Publishing Company

All rights reserved. No part of this work may be reproduced or transmitted in any form or by any means, electronic or mechanical, including photocopying or recording, or by any information storage and retrieval system, without the prior written permission of the copyright owner unless such copying is expressly permitted by federal copyright law. Requests for permission to make copies of any part of the work should be addressed to Houghton Mifflin Harcourt Publishing Company, Attn: Contracts, Copyrights, and Licensing, 9400 Southpark Center Loop, Orlando, Florida 32819-8647.

Printed in USA

ISBN: 978-0-544-07326-5

3 4 5 6 7 8 9 10 1083 21 20 19 18 17 16 15 14

4500470116 A B C D E F G

If you have received these materials as examination copies free of charge, Houghton Mifflin Harcourt Publishing Company retains title to the materials and they may not be resold. Resale of examination copies is strictly prohibited.

Possession of this publication in print format does not entitle users to convert this publication, or any portion of it, into electronic format.

# Contents

Introduction . . . . . . . . . . . . . . . . . . . . . . . . . . . . . 3
Cars Use Different Kinds of Energy . . . . . . . . . . . 4
Chemical Energy Runs Cars . . . . . . . . . . . . . . . . . 6
Electrical Energy Runs Cars . . . . . . . . . . . . . . . . . 8
Cars Use Heat and Thermal Energy . . . . . . . . . . . 10
Cars Use Sound and Light Energy . . . . . . . . . . . . 11
Cars Convert Energy . . . . . . . . . . . . . . . . . . . . . 12
Cars Use Conductors and Insulators . . . . . . . . . . 13
Responding . . . . . . . . . . . . . . . . . . . . . . . . . . . . 14
Glossary . . . . . . . . . . . . . . . . . . . . . . . . . . . . . . 15

## Vocabulary

energy
heat
potential energy
kinetic energy
mechanical energy
electrical energy

chemical energy
thermal energy
conductor
insulator

## Stretch Vocabulary

internal-combustion engine
cylinder
piston
spark plug
crankshaft
efficiency
hybrid car

# Introduction

Welcome to the auto tour! This isn't a tour of the latest car models or cars from the past. It's about what's *inside* a car, under the hood, where the real action takes place. In other words, it's about energy.

A car is a large machine with many connected parts. Different types of cars have different features. But they all have one important thing in common. They all use energy!

On this tour, you'll learn how cars use different kinds of energy. For example, you'll learn how gasoline and electricity provide energy to engines. You'll also see how one form of energy changes into another. You'll even observe how energy provides heat, light, and sound in a car. Get your ticket and come along!

Ever since they were first invented, cars have been fueled by different forms of energy.

# Cars Use Different Kinds of Energy

Let's start by talking about energy. How does a car start? It's easy, right? A driver gets in the car, turns the key, puts a foot on the gas pedal, and goes! But what actually makes the car move?

Energy is what makes a car move. Energy is the ability to cause changes in matter. Any movement is a change—so anything that moves has energy. Picture a car parked at the curb. The car isn't moving. But even in this position, the car has energy. It has potential energy, the energy that an object has because of its position or its condition. Potential energy is also known as stored energy.

Now, imagine that the driver turns the key and puts a foot on the gas pedal. The car begins to move. The car now has kinetic energy, the energy of motion. The faster the car moves, the more kinetic energy it has.

So, the potential energy in a standing car becomes kinetic energy when the car begins to move. When potential and kinetic energy come together, the result is mechanical energy.

Driving involves starting, speeding up, slowing down, and stopping. When a car starts and moves, it has kinetic energy, or movement. When the car approaches a red light, it slows down and stops. Then the kinetic energy becomes potential energy again.

Next, let's talk about a car's battery and energy. Turning the key in the car's starter turns on the battery. The battery starts the engine and connects to the electrical system. Electrical energy provides electricity to parts of the car. For example, electrical energy turns on the lights, plays the radio, and makes the windshield wipers work. If a car battery has lost its charge, the car won't start. The battery can be recharged, but sooner or later it will have to be replaced.

This is a standard car battery. A mechanic can determine if it is charged or if it needs to be replaced.

A car also has an engine. The purpose of the engine is to burn fuel that will move the car. When fuel burns, a chemical reaction changes the chemicals and produces chemical energy. Chemical energy changes to kinetic energy when the car moves.

Now let's learn more about how a car's engine works.

# Chemical Energy Runs Cars

A car's engine is a machine that changes the chemical energy in fuel into kinetic energy. Most cars today have an internal combustion engine. In this type of engine, the fuel is burned inside the engine.

Here's what happens when a driver turns on a car engine. Tiny drops of gasoline mix with air. Air contains oxygen, which is necessary for the gasoline to burn. This gas and air mixture moves into a cylinder, or tube, in the engine. A valve, or opening, at the top of the cylinder opens, and the mixture flows in.

Inside the cylinder, there is a piston. This part moves up and down and causes other parts of the engine to move. The piston moves down when the gas-air mixture moves in. Then the valve at the top closes so that the mixture can't get out.

Next, the piston rises up in the tube. This movement tightly squeezes the gas and air mixture. Another part, the spark plug, is located at the top of the cylinder. This part creates a spark, or flame. The spark sets the fuel on fire. This creates an explosion in the cylinder. The force of the explosion pushes the piston down.

The piston then goes back to the top of the cylinder. The valve opens and releases the exhaust from the burning gases. Then the steps in this cycle of events start over again.

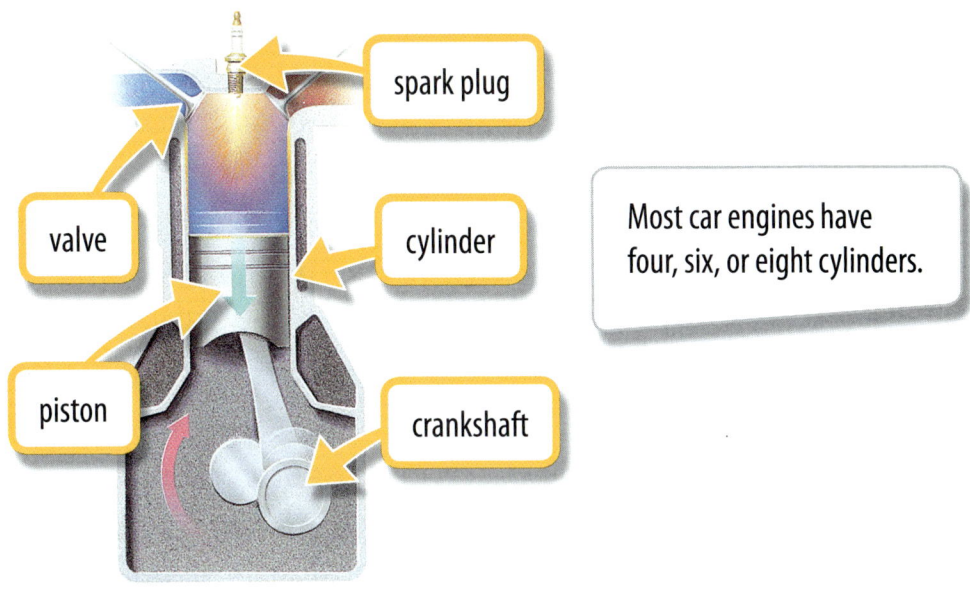

Most car engines have four, six, or eight cylinders.

The piston is also connected to a crankshaft. This long metal piece connects the engine to the car's wheels and helps turn them. When the piston moves up and down, it causes the crankshaft to turn. The motion turns the car's wheels.

This type of internal-combustion engine is found in most cars. Other types of engines burn fuel outside the engine itself. An example is the steam engine. This engine burns fuel to heat water in a boiler. This creates steam, which is used to turn the car's wheels.

What these engines have in common is that they all use chemical energy. As we continue on our tour, we'll see an engine that uses a different kind of energy to move a car. Let's go explore the electric car!

## Electrical Energy Runs Cars

An electric car doesn't have an internal-combustion engine, and it doesn't use gasoline as fuel. An electric car gets its energy from electricity that's stored in batteries. It has a motor that turns the wheels on the car. The motor gets its energy from a battery, too. This battery is a bit like the batteries you'd use in a flashlight, but it's a lot larger! Electrical energy is converted to kinetic energy when the car moves.

The batteries used in an electric car lose stored energy after the car has been moving for a while. Then they have to be recharged by plugging the car into an electrical outlet. Some cars can plug right into a regular wall outlet. Others need a larger outlet. Electric cars can also be charged at charging stations.

electric car recharging

The first cars in the early 1900s ran on either steam, gasoline, or electricity. Electric automobiles were the preferred type of car. Gas-fueled cars were noisier and gave off a lot of smelly smoke. They were also hard to start. Drivers had to turn a crank on the front of the car over and over.

By the 1920s, gas-fueled cars had become easier to use and more affordable. New and better roads meant that people were driving longer distances. Electric cars could travel only short distances before they needed to be recharged.

Today, concerns about pollution and the cost of gasoline have led to a new interest in electric cars. Electric cars give off little pollution in the form of exhaust. They are also more efficient; they waste less energy than gas-fueled cars do.

There are still problems with electric cars. They can go only about 160–190 kilometers (100–120 miles) before they need to be recharged. Recharging the large battery takes several hours. But scientists are working to improve the cars. One development has been the hybrid car. Hybrids use both a gasoline engine and an electric, battery-operated motor. The running motor keeps recharging the battery pack, so the driver does not have to depend on electrical outlets to recharge it. Hybrid cars have better fuel efficiency, and they are less polluting than cars that use gas. Drivers can travel many more miles on one tank of gas.

## Cars Use Heat and Thermal Energy

Who wants to drive in a cold, unheated car? You may be wondering where the heat in a car comes from. First the driver has to start the car. That gets the battery, the engine, and the electrical system going. Next, the driver turns a switch on the dashboard that sends a signal to the system. The air in the heater warms up and moves to the inside of the car, where the air is cooler.

In an electric car, this process happens because electrical energy can change to heat energy. Heat is the energy that moves between objects of different temperatures. In gas-fueled cars, the heat energy comes from fuel burned in the engine. When heat moves, heat energy always moves from warmer to cooler objects.

## Cars Use Sound and Light Energy

It's fun to enjoy the sounds of a radio, CD, or MP3 player in a car, but sound also plays an important role in automobile safety.

Sounds are made when something vibrates, or moves back and forth. These vibrations, or movements, make sound waves. The sound waves move through the air and reach our ears. Sound waves from a car's horn warn a pedestrian or another driver of a dangerous situation.

Lights are another essential feature of a car. Headlights are necessary at night or in bad weather so that drivers can see. Lights also help to make a car more visible to other drivers. Brake lights, located in the rear of the car, are one of an automobile's most important safety features. When a driver pushes the brake pedal, the lights go on and warn cars behind that the driver is slowing down or stopping. Hazard lights flash on and off to let others know that a driver is in some sort of danger. Signal lights warn other drivers when a car ahead of them is about to turn right or left.

How do these lights work? The push or the flick sends a message to the car's electrical system. Electrical energy turns on the lights.

# Cars Convert Energy

There's a lot of energy moving around a car. These forms of energy don't work on their own, or separate from each other. One form of energy can be converted, or changed, into another form. Here are a few ways that cars convert energy.

A car is parked at the top of a hill. When the brake is released, the car begins to roll down the hill. Potential, or stored, energy changes to kinetic energy, or movement. This energy change takes place every time a car stops and starts.

A driver starts up a car. Chemical energy stored in the battery changes to electrical energy. All parts of the car that use electricity are ready to go. That includes the heat, the sounds, and the lights!

The engine burns fuel. Chemical energy in the fuel is changed to kinetic energy when the car begins to move. Mechanical energy of the engine is converted into electrical energy to recharge the battery.

Turn on the radio to listen to a football game. Electrical energy is changed to sound energy. Turn on the lights inside the car so you can read a map. Electrical energy is changed to light energy. As you travel in a car, energy changes take place over and over again.

## Cars Use Conductors and Insulators

Wires are part of the electrical system in a car. They transfer electricity. The material in the center of a wire is a metal, such as copper. That's because metal is a good conductor of electricity. A conductor is a material that lets heat or an electrical charge travel through easily. Electricity travels through the metal to parts of the engine, to the sound system, and to the lights.

The material surrounding the metal wire is plastic or rubber. These materials are not good conductors. They're insulators, materials that don't let heat or electricity move through easily. The insulating material makes the electrical wires safe to touch.

That completes the auto tour. The next time someone asks you about how cars use energy, *you* can take them on a tour!

You can see that wires are a basic part of a car's energy system.

13

# Responding

### Make a Data Table

Some types of cars use energy more efficiently than others. These cars can go longer distances on fewer gallons of gasoline. Do research to compare five different cars. Find out how many miles per gallon each car gets in both city and highway driving. Try to compare five very different types of cars, such as an SUV, a small car, a mid-size car, and so on. Organize your data in a three-column table with the heads *Car*, *City*, and *Highway*. Compare your findings with those of your classmates.

### Write a Persuasive Letter

Hybrid cars run on both gasoline and electricity. You get the energy benefits of both systems. Do research to learn more about hybrid cars and how they use energy. Write a persuasive letter to someone in which you try to convince him or her to either buy or not buy a hybrid car.

# Glossary

**chemical energy** [KEM•ih•kuhl EN•er•jee] Energy that can be released by a chemical reaction.

**conductor** [kuhn•DUK•ter] A material that lets heat or electrical charges travel through it easily.

**crankshaft** [KRAYNK•shaft] A long metal tube that connects the engine to a car's wheels and helps turn them.

**cylinder** [SIL•uhn•der] A tube in which fuel is burned in an engine.

**efficiency** [i•FISH•uhn•see] The ability to do something or produce something without wasting materials, time, or energy.

**electrical energy** [ee•LEK•trih•kuhl EN•er•jee] Energy that comes from electric current.

**energy** [EN•er•jee] The ability to cause changes in matter.

**heat** [HEET] The energy that moves between objects of different temperatures.

**hybrid car** [HY•brid KAR] A car that uses both a gasoline engine and an electric battery-operated motor to run.

**insulator** [IN•suh•lay•ter] A material that does not let heat or electricity move through it easily.

15

**internal-combustion engine** [in•TER•nuhl kuhm•BUHS•chuhn EN• jin] An engine in which the fuel is burned within engine cylinders, or tubes.

**kinetic energy** [kih•NET•ik EN•er•jee] The energy of motion.

**mechanical energy** [muh•KAN•ih•kuhl EN•er•jee] The total potential and kinetic energy of an object.

**piston** [PIS•tuhn] A part of an engine that moves up and down inside a tube and causes other parts of the engine to move.

**potential energy** [poh•TEN•chuhl EN•er•jee] Energy that an object has because of the object's position or its condition.

**spark plug** [SPARK PLUHG] A part of an engine that produces a spark that makes fuel burn.

**thermal energy** [THER•muhl EN•er•jee] Energy created by heat.